THE DINOSAUR FEATHER

SCAN THE QR CODE ON THE BACK COVER
TO UNLOCK A SPECIAL MESSAGE FROM
ROBERT IRWIN

D0110451

THE DINOSAUR FEATHER

WRITTEN BY JACK WELLS

RANDOM HOUSE AUSTRALIA

A Random House book
Published by Random House Australia Pty Ltd
Level 3, 100 Pacific Highway, North Sydney NSW 2060
www.randomhouse.com.au

First published by Random House Australia in 2013

Addresses for companies within the Random House Group can be
found at www.randomhouse.com.au/offices

National Library of Australia
Cataloguing-in-Publication Entry

Author: Irwin, Robert, 2003–
Title: The Dinosaur Feather / Robert Irwin, Jack Wells.
ISBN: 978 1 74275 092 7 (pbk.)
Series: Robert Irwin dinosaur hunter; 4.
Target Audience: For primary school age children.
Subjects: Dinosaurs – Juvenile fiction.
Other Authors/Contributors: Harding, David.
Dewey Number: A823.4

Cover and internal illustrations by Lachlan Creagh
Cover and internal design by Christabella Designs
Typeset by Midland Typesetters, Australia
Printed in Australia by Griffin Press, an accredited ISO AS/
NZS 14001:2004 Environmental Management System printer

Random House Australia uses papers that are natural, renewable and
recyclable products and made from wood grown in sustainable forests.
The logging and manufacturing processes are expected to conform to
the environmental regulations of the country of origin.

CHAPTER ONE

The humid Queensland air stuck to Robert's face like vegemite at lunchtime. Gently, he pulled back the fern he was hiding behind. He wanted to get a better look at the creature.

'She's a real beauty,' he whispered. 'Almost 2 metres tall and pretty heavy.

Believe it or not, these wonderful animals can run up to 50 kilometres an hour. They can jump and swim too.'

He squatted down but stretched his neck over the plant's soft, leafy fronds.

'Usually they are shy, solitary creatures,' he said, 'but when they're frightened, you'd better watch out! The name we gave this one says it all: Stomp!'

It was then that Robert leant too heavily on the light branch he was holding. He lost his balance and fell forwards into the moist and dirty leaf

litter, hitting the ground with a *thud*.
Someone laughed from a short distance away and a startled Stomp the cassowary dashed off into the scrub.

'Cut!' said the director.

The camera operator and sound recordist sighed and lowered their heavy equipment.

Robert turned to his best friend. 'Crikey, Riley,' he said, getting to his feet, 'you have to be quiet. It could take ages to find Stomp again.'

'No way,' said Riley. 'Those birds are massive.'

Robert began brushing dirt and wet leaves off his khaki pants and shirt. 'But they're really shy.'

'Oh, sorry,' chuckled Riley. 'I couldn't help it. You should have seen your face when you fell. It was hilarious.'

The two friends smiled. Robert could never stay cross at Riley for long. He told himself for the millionth time how lucky he was to live at Australia Zoo and tell visitors about cassowaries and the other amazing animals that lived there.

Robert's mother Terri and older sister Bindi walked over from where they had been watching the film shoot. 'Great job, Robert,' said his mum, 'but stop beating up on the tree ferns!' She gave him a warm smile. 'I can see you'll be as great on TV as your father.'

'And your sister!' said Bindi, tickling her little brother around his waist.

Now it was Robert's turn to laugh.

'So, have we finished bird-watching now?' asked Riley. 'I want to go see the crocs!'

Terri chuckled. 'You and Robert are becoming more similar every day. Like two birds of a feather.'

Robert and Riley grinned. They both knew Terri was right.

Simon, who had been directing the film shoot, asked them not to go see the crocs just yet. 'We need to find Stomp again,' he said. 'I have to wrap this shoot today.'

Riley didn't like hearing that. His moan sounded like a roar from one of Australia Zoo's tigers.

'That was awesome, Robert,' Simon said. 'You made the cassowary seem so exciting. It was almost like you were talking about a dinosaur or something.'

Robert's eyes widened. Dinosaurs were his special subject. He was an expert, and one day he hoped to become a palaeontologist. 'It's funny you say that,' he said. 'Birds and dinosaurs have more in common than most people think.'

Simon smiled. 'I'd heard that they call you the Dinosaur Hunter.'

Robert and Riley shared a smile. No-one but the two of them knew just how truthful that name had become.

As it was time for Bindi and Terri to help the keepers feed Graham, their giant crocodile, the camera crew decided to sit in the shade for a 10-minute break.

'Can I go too?' whined Riley.

'We'll meet you at the crocs when you've finished filming,' Bindi answered.

Robert slapped his friend on the back. 'Looks like you're stuck here with me,' he said.

Riley sighed. 'I suppose the crocs won't be going anywhere. Besides, cassowaries are pretty cool too, really.'

Robert nodded in agreement, thinking of the bird's dark black feathers and its bright red and blue decoration.

"They are the third largest bird in the world,' said Robert. 'Only the ostrich and emu are taller.'

Riley picked up a large, flat piece of bark and held it to his head like a shark fin. 'What are those horn things on their heads for?'

Robert grinned. 'They're called *casques*. We're not sure, but they could be for display, protection or even to help cassowaries make their distinctive super-low calls.'

Suddenly, a low, booming sound came from a short distance away within some trees. Robert and Riley spun around and looked at each other.

'Stomp!' they cried.

CHAPTER TWO

The two boys dashed swiftly but quietly through the dense tree area of Australia Zoo. They didn't hear any more cassowary calls, just the high-pitched tweeting and honking of the other birds in the treetops above.

Then there was a rustle in the bushes

a few metres in front of them. Robert motioned to his friend to get down low.

'Is that a cassowary?' squawked Riley.

'Ssh!' said Robert.

Everyone in the Irwin family was good at handling and studying animals, and Robert was no different. He knew that any sudden movements or sounds could frighten away whatever was foraging in the bushes.

They both lay silently on the ground, watching the plants in front of them, waiting for the animal to show itself.

Lying on the ground, Robert could feel his prized possession in his shorts pocket – the fossilised *australovenator* (*oss-tra-low-ven-ah-tor*) claw he always carried with him. He had unearthed it on a fossil dig on his last birthday. Somehow, the claw had managed to transport Robert and Riley back in time to the Age of Dinosaurs. Robert smiled, thinking of all the mind-blowing adventures he'd already had.

Then the familiar long neck of Stomp the cassowary appeared between some plants.

'It's her, all right,' whispered Robert.

'What's she doing?' hissed Riley.

'She's looking for fallen fruit,' said Robert as quietly as he could. 'Cassowaries are mostly frugivorous. That means fruit is their main source of food.'

Stomp found something particularly delicious not far from the boys. They watched her enjoy it before Robert continued. 'Humans have made cassowaries an endangered species by destroying their habitats,' he said. 'The sad thing is, if cassowaries die out, many of the plants in our rainforests will too. Cassowaries help spread their seeds around.'

Riley looked quizzically at Robert. 'How can they do that?' he asked. 'They don't have hands.'

Then Stomp passed a large amount of droppings as she walked in front of their hiding spot.

'That's how,' said Robert.

Riley gave such a disgusted look that Robert had to fight the urge to laugh out loud. 'Come on,' he chuckled. 'We should get the others and try filming again.'

But Riley didn't move. He was in awe of the bird that was larger than him. 'They're definitely big,' he said. 'Imagine how huge their eggs must be!'

'They're about 14 centimetres long, I think,' said Robert. 'Actually, that would be about the same size as some dinosaur eggs.'

'That reminds me, what were you saying before?' asked Riley. 'I mean, birds and dinosaurs can't really be related, can they?'

'Why not?'

'I know cassowaries are big, but dinosaurs were so much bigger.'

'Many dinosaurs were smaller than cassowaries,' said Robert. '*Micropachy-cephalosaurus* (*micro-packy-sef-a-lo-sor-us*) was just over half a metre long. They're one of my favourites. They probably would have even been afraid of our Stomp!'

Riley laughed. 'Micro-*what*-a-saurus? That's a long name for a small dinosaur!'

'I reckon!' Robert smiled. 'It took lots of practice to learn how to say it properly.'

'But I've seen dinosaurs,' said Riley, 'and they look totally different to birds. Dinosaurs didn't have wings or beaks. They didn't even have feathers!'

'Many dinosaurs did have feathers,' said Robert. 'Some had wings, and some had toothless mouths like beaks.'

Stomp was now scratching in the dirt. Her three-toed feet were fearsome to watch in action, especially the long, middle claw on each one.

'There are other similarities too,' said Robert. 'Where else have you seen a claw like that?'

18

'Your *australovenator* claw!' squealed Riley. 'Quick, pull it out – I want to see how it measures up to Stomp's.'

Carefully, Robert slid the claw out of his pocket and held it in front of his face. He lined it up in his vision with the cassowary's claws.

'Let me see,' said Riley. He reached out for the claw, bumping Robert's arm.

'Careful,' whispered Robert, 'it's millions of years old. I don't want to drop it.'

Riley swiped at the claw. His fingers

grabbed at it, clenching both the claw and Robert's hand at the same time.

'Ow! Riley!'

As the claw pricked Robert's palm, he knew his shout had scared Stomp away. He looked up to see the tall cassowary disappear . . . and then everything else did as well. The trees, sky and ground went all wobbly, then vanished and changed. Dizziness took over and the two boys couldn't tell which way was up.

CHAPTER THREE

When Robert opened his eyes, he and Riley were still lying on the ground, surrounded by trees. Nothing much had changed.

Then Riley spoke. 'Is it just me or did it get a little chilly all of a sudden?'

It had. A moment ago Robert had been sweating in the heat. 'Yes,' said

Robert, blowing air into his hands. 'And look, these plants aren't the kinds we have at home.'

'This isn't Australia Zoo any more, is it?' asked Riley.

Robert shook his head. His claw had surely transported them to another prehistoric dinosaur habitat. 'I wonder where we are, though. And when!'

They stood up and walked cautiously through the thinly forested area, rubbing their bare arms to try to warm up. Now they weren't worried about staying hidden from cassowaries. From experience, they thought carnivorous dinosaurs might be the real threat here.

They scanned their surroundings for anything dangerous as they walked. After a minute or two, Robert held up his hand. 'Stop,' he whispered. 'Look in the clearing over there.'

Riley squinted into the distance. 'Dinosaurs!' he said.

'Right,' said Robert. 'A *Segnosaur* (seg-no-sore)! That means only one thing.' He placed the magic claw back into his shorts pocket and pulled out the other object he never left home

without – his digital voice recorder. Robert quickly pressed record. 'We have arrived in the late Cretaceous period, maybe 75 million years ago. Some *segnosaurs* are drinking from a stream in the distance. That means we are probably somewhere in Central Asia.'

Somehow the claw had taken them to a whole new continent!

'Awesome,' said Riley. 'But it's just like I told you – dinosaurs don't have feathers or wings. Even from this distance I can see that.'

Robert squinted to see the reptiles better in the glare of the midday sun.

'Birds are thought to have evolved from theropods, not *segnosaurs*.'

'Do you think we might meet some theropods or feathered dinosaurs here?'

'There's a good chance,' said Robert. 'Most of the fossils found of feathered dinosaurs have been uncovered in China.'

A couple of *segnosaurs* had stopped lapping at the stream and were beginning to walk away on their four powerful limbs. They reminded Robert of the big crocs back home that Riley had been so desperate to see. 'It's funny,' he said, 'scientists now know that *Tyrannosaurus rex* had just as much in common with birds as with reptiles like crocs or alligators.'

Riley shook his head. 'I don't know, mate,' he said. 'You're my best friend and you know so much more about animals than I do, but I'm not sure if I'll believe that until I see it for myself.'

'Fair enough,' replied Robert.

'Look around you,' continued Riley. 'There are no feathered dinosaurs, just the *segnosaurs* and that giant bird sitting in its nest over there.'

Robert's ears tingled. 'Giant bird?' he echoed. 'Where?'

Riley pointed back in the direction they had come. 'See? It's sitting in a nest among all the trees.'

'But, Riley,' shouted Robert as he jumped around excitedly, 'that isn't a bird!'

'What are you talking about?'

Robert placed his voice recorder close to his mouth. 'Riley has just pointed out an *Oviraptor* (o-vee-rap-tor) sitting in its nest,' he said slowly. 'A dinosaur completely covered in colourful feathers!'

CHAPTER FOUR

Riley gasped. 'Crikey!'

'You took the words right out of my mouth,' said Robert. 'This is awesome!'

The two boys walked back towards the *oviraptor*. As they got closer, they crept on all fours, trying to get as near to the dinosaur as they dared.

The dinosaur was sitting in a large nest on the ground, spreading its feathered arms over its eggs for protection. Robert had to admit the arms looked a lot like wings. He had to keep reminding himself that *oviraptors* were dinosaurs – reptiles – and not birds.

They stopped and tried to get a better look through the plants that surrounded the *oviraptor*. 'This is close enough,' said Robert.

Riley agreed. 'I don't need her thinking we're after her eggs.'

30

Robert studied the *oviraptor*. 'To tell you the truth, I don't know if that's a she or a he.'

Riley shot his friend a confused glance. 'What do you mean? She's a mum sitting in her nest!'

'But rules aren't strict in the animal world,' said Robert. 'I mean, with cassowaries, it's the male who looks after the eggs and the chicks.'

Riley put his hands on his hips. 'Am I going crazy? Dinosaurs that look like birds, dads acting like mums. What's next? Fish running a marathon?'

Robert laughed. 'Just keep your voice down. Whether it's a male or female *oviraptor*, I don't want to bother it!'

Riley continued rubbing his cold arms while Robert spoke into his recorder again. 'The *oviraptor's* arms are short and feathered. We can't see the tail. I hope to see it feed with its powerful beak while we're here.'

'I was sure it was a bird,' whispered Riley. 'It isn't as big as other dinosaurs. It isn't even as big as a cassowary. And it has that thing on its head like cassowaries do too.'

Robert spied another glance at the *oviraptor*. Riley was right. How had he not noticed the dome on its head before? The similarities between the two animals were amazing, even though one was a reptile, the other a bird, and they lived 75 million years apart!

The *oviraptor* buried its head under an arm to take a snooze. Robert and Riley just stared at it, almost in the open now, less worried of being noticed. They warmed their hands in their pockets as they watched.

'I guess the feathers keep them warm,'

said Robert. 'I'm sure the *oviraptor* isn't feeling the cold like we are.'

'True.'

'Lots of dinosaurs had feathers,' Robert continued. '*Khaan*, *mononykus*, and one of my favourites: the beautiful *caudipteryx*.'

'Fine,' sighed Riley, 'but I know none of the famous dinosaurs like *velociraptor* or *tyrannosaurus* had feathers.'

Robert raised an eyebrow but said nothing.

Riley stopped. 'No way!' he cried.

'Yep! *Tyrannosaurus* and *velociraptor* are both believed to have had feathers.'

Robert laughed. 'At least on some parts of their bodies, or when they were babies.'

'I don't believe this!' shouted Riley. 'I get whizzed back in time, there are feathered dinosaurs, it's freezing, and – and – *aa-choo!*'

'Now the *oviraptor* is staring at us!' said Robert, alarmed. 'Quick, let's get out of here!'

CHAPTER FIVE

But they couldn't run. Their feet were frozen, and it wasn't just because it was cold. Partly through fear, partly in amazement, the two boys stood like statues and stared at the *oviraptor* as it raised itself up on its two long legs.

'Look,' said Robert, pointing at the tip

of the *oviraptor's* tail. 'There's another reason for having feathers: presentation.'

The *oviraptor* fanned out the beautiful, long feathers on the tip of its tail, almost like a peacock might do. Then it made a loud squealy, squawky sound that echoed all around them.

'That's all the presentation I need to see,' said Riley. 'I'm out of here!'

Riley turned and ran into the cover of the denser trees behind them. Robert was quick to follow, but in the back of his mind he knew they could never outrun an *oviraptor*.

Robert kept looking back as they skipped over tree roots and plants. The *oviraptor* was only about as tall as they were, but it had a sharp beak and claws.

The dinosaur ran after them for a little way, but then stopped, seemingly happy to see the egg thieves scared off.

Robert called out to his friend to stop running, but Riley didn't until he had found protection behind a large tree.

He was breathing heavily as Robert ran around to join him. They stood for a moment, leaning on the trunk and catching their breath. Robert saw they were at the top of a hill. It was quite steep and he couldn't see the bottom, thanks to the small plants and trees that grew all over it.

Once he'd caught his breath, he took out his voice recorder. 'The *oviraptor* was very protective of its nest,' said Robert into the microphone. 'We will do our best to stay clear of any more of them.'

Then he looked down. Lying at the foot of the tree, between two roots, was a round, smooth and lightly coloured object. 'Hey, Riley, look!' he said.

'Whoa! Is that an egg? A dinosaur egg?'

Robert picked it up gently and turned to face Riley. 'It's big but not gigantic. I can hold it in my palm,' he said. 'I wonder if it's from an *oviraptor's* nest?'

'But what's it doing here?'

Their breathing quickened again, this time from excitement. They knew how lucky they were to be holding an actual prehistoric egg. 'I don't know,' said Robert, cradling the egg in his palm, 'but its home must be close by.'

Robert and Riley looked at each other. They both knew the egg might have been lying there for days, but they couldn't just leave it.

'If it *is* the *oviraptor's* egg,' said Riley, 'I'm not going back there. I don't want to be screeched at again. I'm not a fan of running for my life!'

'At least it warmed us up a bit,' said Robert with a smile.

'Being warm is nice, but being safe is better,' said Riley.

'Mate, there's nothing to worry about,' reassured Robert. 'We'll just creep back towards the nest and wait in hiding for a glimpse of the eggs. If they match, we'll slip it in while the *oviraptor* sleeps.'

Riley was still leaning with his back and hands on the tree, looking down the steep hill. 'You're sure we'll be safe?'

'Yes.' Robert nodded. 'Just don't sneeze this time.'

Just then an *oviraptor* reappeared from around the tree, opened its beak and squealed at full volume in Robert's face.

Robert jumped, almost dropping the egg. Riley screamed in terror before stepping away from the tree, tripping on some roots and rolling down the long, dirty hill.

CHAPTER SIX

'Aaah! Robert!' cried Riley as he rolled away. 'Save me!'

Riley's shouting startled the beautiful but fierce *oviraptor*. It shrieked and ran away, leaving Robert alone but shaken.

He held the egg in both hands like a priceless gem and approached the top of the hill. Looking down, he couldn't see Riley any more, though the constant yelping told Robert that his friend was scared but unhurt.

'Don't worry, mate,' Robert's voice echoed into the valley, 'I'm coming!'

Robert made his way down the hill with sideways steps, ensuring his boots were firmly placed before taking each step. If he tripped, not only might he get hurt, but the egg would probably be crushed.

In no time at all, Robert was most of the way down and leaning on a thin tree.

From there he could see Riley, who had stopped rolling and was sitting at the bottom of the hill. 'Stay there, I'm on my way,' Robert called.

Riley looked up the slope and gave Robert the 'okay' sign. 'I guess that was one way to escape a protective *oviraptor*,' he chuckled as he patted his legs clean.

But Robert didn't come. He was pointing over Riley's shoulder in alarm.

'What's wrong?' puzzled Riley. He turned and stared straight into the eyes of another wild *oviraptor*.

Riley turned and began clambering back up the hill on all fours. Dirt flew everywhere. A dust cloud covered the *oviraptor's* densely feathered body. It swiped its domed head at Riley's legs as he crawled up the hill, but missed.

Robert laid the egg on the ground within a large, fallen leaf. He stretched an arm down towards Riley while holding onto the trunk of the thin tree. As soon as Riley was close enough, Robert grabbed his hand and pulled him up behind the tree. The *oviraptor* gave out a shrill call from below.

48

'I think I've seen enough feathered dinosaurs to last me a lifetime,' said Riley, panting hard.

'It's okay,' said Robert. 'It won't be following you up. Look!'

A small group of two-legged dinosaurs emerged from within the trees at the base of the hill and approached the *oviraptor*. These dinosaurs were similar in size to the *oviraptor* but they didn't have feathers. They hissed at the *oviraptor*, who squealed back at them before deciding to leave the newcomers in peace.

'Please tell me these ones won't eat us,' said Riley, watching from above.

'They won't. They're herbivores,' said Robert.

Riley sat down in relief. 'What kind of dinosaurs are they?' he asked. 'I owe those little guys my thanks.'

'I think they're *micropachycephalosauruses*,' said Robert, excitedly.

'Of course, the dinosaurs with the name longer than they are,' said Riley. 'But today is Topsy-turvy Day so why should I be surprised?'

CHAPTER SEVEN

The two young dinosaur hunters looked down from either side of the tree. Robert watched in awe as a group of one of his favourite ancient reptiles foraged for plants to eat.

He remembered the first time he had heard about the *micropachy-*

cephalosaurus. On his last birthday, while digging for fossils for the Australian Age of Dinosaurs museum, Robert had seen a drawing of one. Immediately after realising he would have been taller than a *micropachycephalosaurus*, it became one of Robert's favourite dinosaurs. After all, he had already fed crocodiles longer than they were! As interesting as cassowaries were, filming a video about a metre-long *micropachycephalosaurus* at Australia Zoo was Robert's dream.

'It's funny that we're on a hill,' said Robert.

'It's not that funny if you roll down it,' said Riley, rubbing his leg.

'No, I mean the first *micropachy-cephalosaurus* fossil was found in China on a cliff.' Robert paused and turned to his friend. 'Maybe this is the place.'

Robert's fingers stretched across the shell of the smooth egg that was now safely back in his hands. He wanted to keep it warm in the hope of saving any baby dinosaur that may be growing inside. Watching the small dinosaurs, Robert wondered if the egg might belong to one of them.

'Riley, have you seen any dinosaur nests around here?' he asked.

Riley took his eyes off the dinosaurs for a moment. 'No, why?'

'I'm just trying to figure out who owns this egg.' Robert held the egg carefully in one hand as he pulled out his voice recorder. 'We have discovered a small pack of *micropachycephalosauruses,*' he said. 'Probably a family group. They are eating leaves off smaller plants. They are definitely shorter than *oviraptors.* I reckon they could run pretty fast.'

'Speaking of running,' said Riley, 'here they come!'

Some of the small dinosaurs were coming up the hill and towards the boys to try a clump of fresh leaves growing on a nearby plant.

Riley looked a little nervous. 'You're positive they aren't meat-eaters?' he asked again.

'Yeah,' said Robert. 'Watch, they prefer salad.'

Two *micropachycephalosauruses* were bickering over the leaves. They were now less than 5 metres from the boys. Robert was certain the dinosaurs must have been aware of their presence by now. Maybe they didn't mind being watched?

'They're amazing,' said Riley, 'but I'm starting to get cold again. Maybe we should try to get home.'

'Y-y-yeah –' said Robert.

The whole world was vibrating. Something large had fallen on the ground nearby, shaking the leaves in the tree above the boys' heads. Then the ground shook again, and again. Robert almost dropped the egg before whipping his other hand over the top of it for safety.

Suddenly, from somewhere in the valley below, came a shriek that made the entire group of *micropachycephalosauruses* turn and run at full pace up the hill, past Robert and Riley.

Robert guessed that not too far away, a large meat-eater had just made lunch out of one of their brothers or sisters. And whatever enjoyed eating them probably wouldn't mind snacking on small humans either.

'We better run,' yelled Robert. 'Now!'

Riley didn't need any encouragement. He jumped down and started pumping his legs as fast as they could carry him up the hill. 'Whatever it is,' he panted, 'I hope it only wants to eat salad!'

CHAPTER EIGHT

The boys knew they would feel safer on higher ground. The denser plants that they had found around the *oviraptor* nest would give them more of a chance to hide too. But running up the hill was a lot harder than rolling down it.

Whatever giant beast was approaching,

feeding on a *micropachycephalosaurus* hadn't slowed it down much. Robert and Riley felt each of its footfalls as they climbed higher.

'What do you think it is?' asked Riley. His cheeks were turning pink from the cold.

'I'm not sure,' said Robert, 'but judging from the vibrations we can feel, it's big.'

Robert and Riley stumbled a few times but slowly rose upwards. Whenever they got close to a plant or tree Riley would grab it to steady himself.

It was even harder for Robert, who had to climb without using his hands. He held the egg with a firm but gentle grip.

Finally, Robert's foot fell flat on the top of the hill. 'Quick, let's find a hiding place,' he wheezed.

'Look,' shouted Riley, 'there's the tree you found the egg under.' He was pointing to his right, which meant that to their left was where they first appeared in late Cretaceous Asia. The nesting *oviraptor* was in that direction too.

They ran straight ahead, under the cover of the trees and plants. Robert looked up at the treetops as he ran, while Riley looked for any evidence of angry, nesting *oviraptors*.

'Find a good tree to climb,' said Robert. 'I want to have a better view of what's coming.'

Riley squealed. 'But the higher you are, the closer to the dinosaur's mouth you'll be!'

'Not necessarily,' said Robert, testing a foot on a strong branch. 'I'll only watch for a moment anyway. I just want to see what it is.'

As Robert searched, Riley stopped

and hugged himself for warmth. 'I just hope it doesn't come this way at all,' he said.

Robert ended up deciding on a tree at the top of the hill, next to the one they had found the egg under. It had regular, strong branches that would be easy to climb. It would also give him a good view of the valley.

Robert tucked his shirt into his pants and gently lowered the egg down his front. It felt warm against his stomach. Then he reached high for a branch and pulled himself up.

Soon Robert had climbed as high as he could go and Riley was looking up at him wide-eyed from about three metres below.

'Just be careful,' whispered Riley. 'Don't fall.'

Robert laughed. 'Don't worry, I don't really want dinosaur egg yolk down my pants!'

They didn't have long to wait. The sound of footsteps told Robert that the mystery dinosaur was coming closer.

With each passing second its footsteps grew louder. Robert's eyes were glued to the treetops, waiting for a glimpse of the mystery dinosaur.

Robert could sense that the predator wasn't trying to walk up the hill, but was walking around it. A moment later, he got his first look at the head of the dinosaur. Next, Robert saw its neck, shoulders and arms as it climbed higher. 'Riley!' he shouted. 'Check it out!'

'No, I don't want to,' Riley called from the base of the tree. 'No way. I've had enough.' Riley hugged the tree trunk tightly and shut his eyes.

Suddenly, looking between the leaves

65

just to the right, Robert could see the entire creature from head to toe. It was now about 50 metres away, and on the same ground level as the boys. It seemed to be looking for something. 'Mate, you must see this!' Robert whispered to Riley.

He saw Riley open one eye just a crack as he clung to the tree like a koala. But once he had caught a glimpse of the 'saur, Riley swung around to get a proper look. 'Whoa!'

The dinosaur was large – perhaps 9 metres long. Its head was big too, with a small horn on its forehead and two large nostrils on top of its snout. The dinosaur yawned, showing long sharp teeth. It should have been one of the most fearsome reptiles the boys had ever seen, but the fact that it was covered from head to toe in long, thick feathers somehow made it seem more cuddly than scary.

'Is that a *tyrannosaurus rex*,' asked Riley, 'or the biggest bird of all time?'

Robert pictured a *tyrannosaurus* in his mind. This dinosaur was a bit smaller and its arms were longer, but Robert agreed it was very similar to a T-rex. It was then that he realised exactly what it was. 'It's *tyrannosaurus's* cousin,' he said, looking down at Riley. 'It's called *Yutyrannus* (yu-ti-ran-us). The name means "feathered tyrant".'

Robert pulled his voice recorder out with his free hand. 'We're standing very close to a *yutyrannus*. Can you believe it?' he whispered. 'The largest dinosaur fossil ever found with visible feathers was one of them.'

The *yutyrannus* began walking again, towards them. The cold breeze picked up, making its feathers ripple like a wave rolling in at the beach.

Robert turned off the recorder. 'Uh-oh, I think we're about to have a visitor.'

Riley yelped. 'What! Make way, I'm coming up too,' he said, scrambling to climb the tree before the feathered tyrant could step on him.

CHAPTER NINE

Riley joined Robert in the tree, standing one branch below him. 'Do you think it's coming to eat us?' he whispered.

'I'm not sure,' said Robert. 'I think it's looking for something.'

'Maybe it's lost an egg,' suggested Riley.

71

Robert felt the egg through his shirt. 'I don't think so,' he said. 'It's too little to be an egg laid by a dinosaur that size.'

The *yutyrannus* walked closer, brushing past branches and leaves as it came. Its face, with coloured, wavy feathers between its eyes, was heading straight for the boys. With each step, the feathered beast caused the tree to vibrate slightly. Soon, it was close enough that it could have reached out and knocked them down.

Then it stopped again. Robert's heart was beating so hard he could feel his pulse in his hands as he gripped the tree. Riley was still and silent just below him.

The *yutyrannus* looked up and around. Whatever it was searching for was high off the ground. It turned, and Robert saw its long tail swing round. Robert could have reached out and touched it. He wondered what its long, bird-like feathers felt like.

But he couldn't risk it.

'I think it's leaving,' whispered Robert.

And then the *yutyrannus* jumped and turned. The ground shook like an earthquake as the dinosaur opened its mouth and screamed into Robert's face. The sound, coming from a mouth that was big enough to chomp him up, was long and loud. *Yutyrannus* saliva streamed off the sharp teeth within its jaws, blown by its warm, foul-smelling breath. Then Riley started screaming too. Robert's ears rang as his face was covered in sticky, slimy spit.

He was scared, but the birds in the surrounding trees were even more afraid. Hundreds of them appeared, chirping in fear as they flew into the

sky – a grey and white flapping cloud.

The *yutyrannus* extended its neck, head and teeth upwards, trying to catch as many of the birds as it could between its dagger-like teeth. It caught and ate many before bounding off, following the flock across the thinly forested landscape of ancient Asia.

Once it was quiet again, Robert let out a deep breath. He peered down to see Riley looking up at him with a pale, wet face. His mouth and eyes were hanging open. 'B-b-birds?' he finally stuttered.

'I know!' said Robert. 'Thank goodness. I thought I was the one about to be eaten for dessert.'

Riley shook his head. 'No, I mean, what are birds doing here?'

'What do you mean? Birds aren't that rare.' Robert laughed. 'You saw a huge cassowary just today, remember?'

'I know, but I thought you said birds evolved from dinosaurs,' said Riley.

'Yes,' said Robert, 'but by the late Cretaceous period birds were already here. All kinds of animals existed together, just like in the 21st century.'

And then Robert's brain clicked. 'Oh wow, how could we not have thought of that before?' he cried.

'What?' asked Riley.

'I know where the egg is from,' said Robert, shimmying down the tree.

Riley followed him down as quickly as he could. 'Really? Where?'

Robert's feet had only touched solid ground for a second before he struggled to climb up a neighbouring tree, the one they had found the egg underneath. Until a moment ago it had been full of the large birds.

'Now where are you going?' called Riley from below.

Robert climbed fast. Soon he had found what he was looking for. Propped firmly within two prongs of a long branch was a nest. Robert climbed onto the branch and lay on it with his arms curved around its thick wood. He held the egg carefully in one hand as he shimmied towards the nest. His eyes peered over the rim of it and inside he saw a small collection of eggs. They were the same size, shape and colour as the one he had been protecting.

'Riley!' he called out. 'I found the egg's home!'

Softly, Robert placed the egg within the nest. He didn't know if a chick was growing inside, or even if the neighbouring eggs contained its brothers and sisters, but he had done the best he could. And surely sitting in a nest was better than lying on the ground all alone.

'A bird's egg!' Riley laughed, once Robert had climbed down. 'It was a simple bird's egg this whole time!'

'I know! Sometimes the easiest explanation is the right one, I guess,' said Robert. Then he noticed something new. 'Uh, Riley, what's that behind your ear?'

'Oh,' said Riley, pulling out a long feather from the side of his face, 'I found a feather from the *yutyrannus*. I thought I'd keep it as a souvenir.'

Robert looked his friend up and down. It had been quite an adventure. They were both covered in a collection of dirt, tree bark and *yutyrannus* saliva. 'Come on,' he said, 'let's get cleaned up and find a way home!'

CHAPTER TEN

The *segnosaurs* Robert and Riley had seen drinking from the stream when they first arrived were gone. The ancient water trickled past them, cold but refreshing. Robert and Riley splashed the chilled water all over their faces.

But it wasn't enough to budge the dirt,

so they completely dunked their grubby heads into the cold water.

Surprisingly, the water wasn't cold after all. In fact, opening his eyes, Robert could feel that the whole world had warmed up a lot.

Then there was a rustle from some bushes nearby. Riley grabbed his friend's arm. 'What's that?' he asked.

They laid low and watched. Then a creature came into view. It wasn't another dinosaur, but it was one of their ancestors: Stomp the cassowary!

'We're back,' laughed Robert.

They got up, glad to be home, and went to find the camera crew.

'You know, it's amazing how much dinosaurs and cassowaries have in common,' said Riley as they walked.

'The main similarity isn't a good one,' said Robert. 'One day those beautiful birds could be extinct too.'

Riley stroked his *yutyrannus* feather a few times before sliding it safely into his pants pocket. 'Well,' he sighed, 'at least we'll never forget them.'

'Boys! Boys! There you are,' called Simon the director, waving them over.

The crew was ready to shoot the video again. It was strange for the two friends to think that they must have only been gone a short while.

'We found Stomp the cassowary,' called Simon. 'She's a few metres behind you, pecking around within those trees. Are you ready to roll?'

Robert was tired, his head spinning with all they had just seen in Asia, 75 million years ago. But he smiled. 'Let's do this,' he said, 'before we lose that feathered tyrant again!'

Drawn by Robert Irwin

MICROPACHYCEPHALOSAURUS

DISCOVERED: 1978 in Shandong Province, China

ETYMOLOGY: Tiny, thick-headed lizard

PERIOD: Late Cretaceous

LENGTH: Approximately half a metre long

WEIGHT: Approximately 5 kilograms

Micropachycephalosaurus is the smallest of all the known pachycephalosaurs. It was bipedal and herbivorous, and currently has the longest generic name of any dinosaur.

YUTYRANNUS

SCIENTIFIC NAME: Yutyrannus huali

DISCOVERED: 2012 in Liaoning Province, China

ETYMOLOGY: Beautiful feathered tyrant

PERIOD: Early Cretaceous

LENGTH: Approximately 9 metres long

HEIGHT: Approximately 3 metres tall

WEIGHT: Approximately 1.4 tonnes

Three almost complete yutyrannus skeletons have been uncovered: an adult, a sub-adult and a juvenile. The fossils were found in Liaoning Province, China, within rocks estimated to be 125 million years old.

Yutyrannus was a large, bipedal predator. A relative of the T-rex, it had relatively long arms with three fingers, and short feet. Its small horn would have added to its fearsome appearance.

Perhaps the most important feature of *yutyrannus* fossils are the visible feathers. *Yutyrannus* is currently the largest dinosaur discovered with clear, fossilised evidence of feathers. Its feathers were as long as 20 centimetres and seem to have covered its entire body. Feathers would have helped *yutyrannus* stay warm in an area with an average temperature of 10 degrees Celsius. It is possible that the feathers were also for decoration, especially the wavy feathers found on their snouts.

FEATHERED DINOSAURS

There is now enough evidence for most scientists to believe that birds evolved from a group of theropod dinosaurs (carnivores that walked on two bird-like feet). The relationship between birds and dinosaurs was discussed as long ago as the 19th century, when the first archaeopteryt fossil was unearthed. Archaeopteryt was a primitive bird that shared many features with dinosaurs.

Scientists predicted the existence of feathered dinosaurs many years before fossils of them began appearing in the 1990s. More continue to be discovered, especially in China, and there are over 30 species of non-flying feathered dinosaurs now known.

Interestingly, feathers are not the main evidence that birds evolved from dinosaurs. From fossils we have learnt that, like birds, many dinosaurs had hollow bones, swallowed stones to help digest their food, built nests, and that they sat on their eggs to warm and protect them. We even know that many dinosaurs slept with their heads under their arms, just like you may have seen a bird sleep with their head under their wing!

Dinosaurs had feathers for a variety of reasons. Some could, perhaps, fly, but mostly they were for staying warm and looking cool to other dinosaurs!

Interested in finding out what Robert does when he's not hunting for dinosaurs?

Check out www.australiazoo.com.au